W9-DJN-749

WHEN THE STARS WROTE BACK

WHEN THE STARS WROTE BACK

poems

TRISTA MATEER

ILLUSTRATED BY
JESSICA CRUICKSHANK

Random House 🏠 New York

Text copyright © 2020 by Trista Mateer
Cover art and interior illustrations copyright © 2020 by Jessica Cruickshank

All rights reserved. Published in the United States by Random House
Children's Books, a division of Penguin Random House LLC, New York.

Random House and the colophon are registered trademarks of
Penguin Random House LLC.

Visit us on the Web! GetUnderlined.com

Educators and librarians, for a variety of teaching tools,
visit us at RHTeachersLibrarians.com

Library of Congress Cataloging-in-Publication Data
Names: Mateer, Trista, author. | Cruickshank, Jessica, illustrator.
Title: When the stars wrote back : poems / Trista Mateer ; illustrated by
Jessica Cruickshank.
Description: First edition. | New York : Random House Children's Books, a
division of Penguin Random House LLC, [2020] | Audience: Ages 14 & up. |
Audience: Grades 10–12.
Identifiers: LCCN 2019053639 (print) | LCCN 2019053640 (ebook) |
ISBN 978-0-593-17267-4 (hardcover) | ISBN 978-0-593-17268-1 (library
binding) | ISBN 978-0-593-17269-8 (epub)
Subjects: LCSH: Young adult poetry, American. | CYAC: Poetry, American. |
LCGFT: Poetry.
Classification: LCC PS3613.A8245 W48 2020 (print) |
LCC PS3613.A8245 (ebook) | DDC 811/.6—dc23

Printed in the United States of America
10 9 8 7 6 5 4 3 2
First Edition

for the stars in you
and the stars in me

CONTENTS

Sometimes I wonder
if signs we want from the universe
are really just signs we want
from ourselves.

WHEN THE
STARS WROTE
BACK

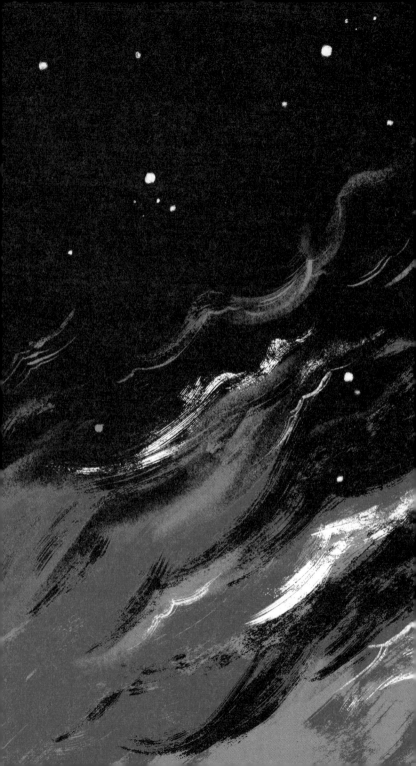

I write EVERYTHING down, but I don't REALLY let anything go.

I am still young and I already forget how to be happy.
I am unkind to myself. I never finish anything I start.
I spend most of my time begging people to stay.

I would do

ALMOST ANYTHING

to shake the taste of

loneliness

loose from my mouth.

STARGAZING

I've been
watching stars
    my whole life

        and not once
        has all that space

            ever made me feel
            anything

                but small.

I THINK I WANT TOO MUCH

Love that crashes like potted plants
    from fifth-story windows.
Love that bursts like an appendix.

Love that is consumed by itself.
Love that thinks only about the NOW NOW NOW.

Love like a floor-to-ceiling map of the world.
Love I keep sticking pushpins in.

Love that doesn't want to hold me back
    from anything
but still won't let go.

He tells me that I am the best thing
and he says it with a grin that tastes like light beer
and 4 a.m. gas station junk food;
it is something sweet, but something empty.

SOME PEOPLE'S ARMS ARE

too easy

TO STAY IN.

A thief in someone else's bed,
I stole a place to lay my head
and meant to be gone in the morning.

I know the boy

is BAD for me

but I hold him

UNTIL my fingers

 BURN.

every night is another dream about car keys / a
half-packed suitcase / passports and plane tickets
/ arrivals gates / crowded train stations / vacant
parking lots / fields of wheat / sunrises in other
cities / smoke spiraling up and away

The truth about love is that I got bored waiting for it.
The truth about love is that I know it doesn't live here
but it's so easy being comfortable.

good things don't last forever
    but bad things have to end too.
good things don't last forever
    but there's still an end for me and you.

You TRIED to make a

GRAVE

out of me

and I ALMOST

LET YOU.

THINGS MY MOTHER TAUGHT ME

1. you are never as good at something
   as you think you are

2. everyone settles eventually

3. under no circumstance
   should you leave the house
   without makeup

4. people can treat you like shit
   and you will still love them

5. you are not pretty enough
   young enough or thin enough;
   you will never be enough

6. boys will be boys
   and there's nothing you can do
   about it

7. your survival depends
   on learning to manipulate people

8. love is the most important thing
   even if it ruins you

THE KINDA BLUES

Like sad but not sad enough.
Like attention seeking.
Like *I dunno, man. Most days she seems fine.*
Like laziness and irritation.
Like anxiety but not full-blown panic.
Like not being able to get out of bed for three days—
but hey, what's three days?
Like never actually writing the last note,
just imagining the lines.
Like it's more of a river and not an ocean
but as far as I'm concerned
you can drown in either one.

My feelings are too big.
Life feels like mud or fog,
maybe quicksand,
a pile of bricks in my bed.

There are days when existing
is exhausting,
when the ache for
a
long
heavy
sleep
is stronger than the
pull
of the sun.

GRAVITY

I swear it's always
the same old shit
holding me down.

I THOUGHT I HAD PERSONAL ISSUES WITH TAKING UP SPACE BUT THEN I REALIZED IT WAS SOCIALLY INGRAINED SEXISM

My brother stands with his legs wide,
with his knees bent
and his arms out

like he's learned to stake a claim
to any space he exists in.

I take up 1/3 of any bed I'm sleeping in
and I never put my things on the seat next to me
on public transit.

I keep trying to make myself small enough
to give other people space to grow.

I was taught how to love
with my whole heart
gutted out
like the inside of a pitted fruit.

I am nothing if not conscientious.
I am nothing if not always making room.

(I am nothing. I am nothing.)

IN WHICH I BERATE MY BODY

who gave you all this permission to want?

My bed is too EMPTY
to sleep in

OR

I am too empty
to SLEEP.

CHERRY COKE ZERO

Mom points at a picture of me and says,
look how much skinnier you used to be.

I think about the year that I packed school lunches
just to throw them out. I think about the time I had
a stomach bug and couldn't keep anything down for
days. How I lost four pounds, and my grandmother
said *oh, good.* I think about the month I ate nothing
but grapefruit. The weeks I drank nothing but green
juice. The days I only consumed vegetable broth. I
think about the dizziness and the lightheadedness,
about being tired all the time. I think about looking
in the mirror and crying. I think about the way I still
don't like to go on dates that involve food because,
somehow, someone seeing me eat still makes me
feel uneasy. I think about Cherry Coke Zero. I think
about the Red Light Green Light diet and about
cutting carbs and about calorie-counting apps. I
think about second-guessing my own body.

She shoves the picture in my face.
I say, *yeah, Mom. I know.*

In the dream,
whenever I open my mouth
I lose all of my teeth.

In the dream,
whenever I open my mouth
I upset my mother.

In the dream,
whenever I open my mouth
I bite down on my tongue.

In the dream,
whenever I open my mouth
I almost say his name.

IN THIS BODY

I was told to be grateful for any attention I could get,
Even when I didn't want it.

Even when it hurt.

You never LEFT A MARK

on my skin.

BUT I FEEL LIKE THERE ARE

scars

EVERYWHERE YOU

touched ME.

IF I AM TO BE

Anything,

LET IT BE

honest.

I wish it had
been your blood
instead of ~~mine~~.

There are two versions of me:

one that forgives like forgiveness is the only thing
they serve here, so I just have to keep ordering it,

and one that doesn't.

The one that doesn't
is the one that writes the poems.

When I couldn't get what I wanted out of life,

I turned to literature:

miles and piles of books,

bouquets of midnight-blue pens.

The page always listened when no one else would.

THE POEM DOES NOT HAVE TO BE GOOD

The poem does not have to be good or noble or beautiful or succinct or long or terrifying or painful. The poem does not have to be kind or angry or about love or about trauma. The poem does not have to be a perfect 10 and it does not have to make strangers laugh or even cry. The poem does not have to resonate with anyone. The poem does not have to be personal or relatable or abstract or pretty. The poem does not have to be book-worthy or journal-worthy. The poem does not have to prove itself to anyone. It doesn't have to be a mirror or a window. It doesn't have to be a miracle.

It just has to say something,
and then take a breath,
and then find the courage to say something else.

People tell me that if I keep writing poetry
about every mouth I meet,
nobody's going to want to kiss me anymore.

But I own everything that ever happens to me
and I refuse to straddle the line between privacy
    and honesty
for the sake of someone else's comfort level.

I will not be a fairy-tale mermaid
willing to give up her own voice for love.

I don't care if they're too loud.

I don't care if they're too truthful.

My poems are shouts disguised as kisses.

My poems are angry and they have a right to be.

The POETRY

never LEAVES me,

even when I

want it to.

The women in my family are always angry about something. The women in my family drink wine with breakfast instead of coffee. The women in my family don't want to talk about it. The women in my family see ghosts everywhere. The women in my family can't decide if birds are a sign of death or luck. The women in my family are secret-keepers. The women in my family never tell the whole truth. They know what the truth does to women. They take everything to the grave.

I don't know
how to keep
my mouth shut.

Always
purging and bingeing.

Always
spilling out words
and then shoving them
back inside.

I dug up my roots a long time ago,
lost all my petals,
and never thought I'd need anything
but thorns.

Love

IS ONE HELL
OF A

quiet burden.

best friends means friends forever / means nights
up late and days together / means walking with
your hand in mine / means letting you steal all
my time / means my whole life is getting better /
means something else now altogether

I was water running strong,
you were stubborn canyon wall.

I _SWORE_ I'D NEVER GET IN

OVER MY HEAD

BUT THE DAY I MET YOU

I WAS *already*

UP TO MY

ANKLES.

This is the OPPOSITE of

SALTING YOUR
WOUNDS;

I want to pour

honey

in them.

~~BIG~~ BANG THEORY

what happens if we collide?
will it feel like atoms bursting?
will it burn like light?
will your hands feel the same as other people's hands?
will the whole world change if we touch?
do you want to find out?

When I thought people
could only want me
in **PIECES**,
I started handing out
SCISSORS.

Kissing her
left me dizzy and breathless
but that wasn't why I did it.

I did it because
it made us both feel less alone
to share a secret

even if I was the secret.

I have daydreams
about the bags under your eyes
and my heart skips
at the mention of your thighs
and I hope when
you fall asleep at night
that you can't rest
without reaching for my side.

My love

is a pair of

SCISSORS

I keep

BEGGING

YOU

not to run with.

NORTH STAR

Suddenly,
your light in my dark.

She put her head on my shoulder and sang to me.
She sang me poetry, she sang me everything.
She made love lyrical.

Please tell me
which part of yourself
you hate **the most**
so I know EXACTLY where
to plant my lips
every time I see you.

I don't like playing games.

I'm always aching to lay my cards down on the table:

You need a 3?

I've got a 3.

Take anything you need.

I get these pains
in my chest
sometimes

like my heart is trying
to beat its way out.

I CAN ALWAYS

feel

ENDINGS COMING

before

THEY GET HERE.

Everyone sees signs of bad weather
before it even hits
and they run for cover.

I wish I had that luxury
but I'm always stuck
in my own storm.

Does it matter why it ended?

Does it make it easier to place blame somewhere?

Do you think the sun sets on everything eventually?

Do you think this was inevitable?

What is it about love that makes it hurt so much to lose?

I sometimes play
too rough
with teeth and claws;

like a dog,
I don't know
when I've gone too far,

bit too hard,
hurt too deep.

I am AFRAID
of ~~speaking~~
AND HEARING

MY MOTHER'S
VOICE.

Sweet thing, soft thing,
girl who used to believe that fairies made skirts
out of her grandmother's lilacs:
what have I done with you?

Girl who used to forgive
until it rubbed her heart raw,
skinned-knees-on-gravel girl.

Girl who got up off the ground
and ran right back in,
girl who slid so hard into home base
she knocked the wind out of herself:
why don't you want to come home?

Why do you keep triple-checking the locks?

When did it get so easy to be hard?
To put the phone down
without texting back?

To scoff at apologies,
toss them aside like fruit pits
and walk away
from whatever might grow?

SIX TEXTS I'M NOT SENDING YOU

1. I miss the sound of your voice. Is it okay to say that?

2. Is it okay to say that I feel like I'm drowning? Both in overdramatic metaphors and in the absence of you? I feel like every day without you in it may as well have been spent at the bottom of my bathtub. I can't hear anything. I can't breathe.

3. It took me a whole week to realize I was getting sick. I thought this was just what it felt like to not be kissing you.

4. I hate that you stopped reading my poems.

5. I'm having a lot of trouble kicking the Big Sad. I keep forgetting to eat. I spend too much time in the shower. I organize my shampoo bottles and knock them all over. I use every kind of soap that I own and I still don't feel clean.

6. I'm not gonna ask you to stay. But I want to.

Sometimes I like to think
you still fall asleep like I do,
reaching out for me
like I keep reaching out for you.

What if I love you forever?
What if it never goes away?
What if I forget my own name
and only remember yours?

I had another in an endlessly long line of dreams
    about you
but I can't remember if we were chasing ghosts or if
    they were chasing us.

My mother refuses to love anything
that doesn't love her back. She
shuns the house cat. Lets her
phone go to voice mail. She
keeps telling me to try it,
says it will be good
for my heart. I
worry it will
shrink
it.

I'm sorry for the things I said.

They weren't eloquent or particularly kind,

but you have to keep in mind:

if I were good at speaking,

I never would have started to write this

all down.

RIGHT NOW

i.   She is smiling in all of her Instagram photos.
I am still writing poetry about her and sharing it
with strangers.

ii.   There are weeks I don't think about her
but then I remember the sound of her laugh
and it ruins me.

iii.   I want to be able to say I've moved on
but I doubt anyone would believe that.

iv.   I don't want to lie.
I want my truths to be worth talking about.

v.   The distance between us is not a competition of
who survives better
but I know she is surviving better.

I deleted every photo
of us from my phone.

Even the ones that
werent of us —
just of me

when we were

HAPPY.

It hurts to remember the reasons I stayed
more than it hurts to remember
the reasons you left.

Love leaves, and look:

something else always comes along that hurts worse,

makes the ache pale in comparison.

WHEN THE BOUGH BREAKS

your childhood best friend sits across from you
at the kitchen table nodding out with a cigarette
in his hands and all you can think about is your
father and why you already know exactly what
heroin looks like in another person's body. you
remember your mother telling you that you can't
make anybody stop doing what they want to do.

the people who get clean are the people who
want to get clean, she said. and you know
it's what she'll say again.

you won't cry on the phone, but your voice
crunches like gravel on the line when you call her.
there's blood in your mouth and all you can think
about are skinned knees, all those games of tag
that led to this moment. there is a tree still in
your grandparents' front yard that always used to
be the safe zone. you wish you could go back to it
right now and press your whole body against it.

I'm ASHAMED of all my

human.

The parts of me that are

SCARED

and

VULNERABLE

and

REAL.

The parts of me that

can be *hurt.*

When my rapist
Super Liked me on Tinder,
I spent an hour looking at his profile pictures

wondering if he was the kind of man
who forgot faces
or remembered them,

wondering which one was worse.

He sits down across from me

   and asks if I ever got my license.

He laughs and says I still look so young.

He says, *I always knew you had a little crush on me.*

He says, *I could have taken advantage of you*

   and I didn't.

Part of me wants to say thank you

but I am training myself to be a bad dog,

   a feral woman.

I say, *you don't get a medal for not being a predator.*

He says, *bitch*

and I show all my teeth.

Is there a way to say it's not my fault
that I keep writing the same poems
about different people?

WHEN THE BOUGH BREAKS AGAIN

You loved the boy and it wasn't enough to stop bad things from happening to him. It was never going to be enough.

He keeps telling you he's going to die and you know he is the bad thing happening to himself and you can't raise a hand to stop it. Can't curl your fingers into a fist big enough. Can't yell loud enough.

You would bend your body into an answer if there were an answer but there isn't one. Only the boy and his sadness and his anger and his shame and your hands, which are feeling more empty by the day.

I'm still trying

to find a way
to forgive myself

for being ALIVE.

Maybe it's time to ease the bite from my words.

Maybe it's time to put my suitcases away.

Maybe it's time to make nice with this town.

Lie down and roll over.

Fear like a

PHANTOM LIMB;

I just can't

shake it.

OLD LOVE

I shake the crumbs of it
out of my sheets / everyone
tells me to stop eating
in bed.

Yes,

THE HEART HEALS
BUT THE HEART HEALS

CROOKED.

I'm afraid of what the poems will look like when I
    stop writing about love.

How cruel they'll get.
How scared.
How unkind.

I don't know when I became a secretive person. There was a time in my life when my mother knew every single thing about me. There was a time when my brother kept all of my secrets close to his chest. I don't know why I stopped trusting him with them. When I cry at night, my mother can't put a name to the things that hurt me. I never meant to hide so much.

I guess I thought
if I SWALLOWED MY SECRETS,
they couldn't swallow
me first.

STARFALL

If I could,
I would hold conversations
with the moon.

I would ask Venus
about loneliness
and Mars about anger.

I would tell the black hole
that I know what it feels like.

I would write letters
to the cosmos;

and when the stars wrote back,
they would say the most dazzling
and necessary things.

Don't dim your light for anyone.

Your existence is meaningful
and necessary

even when you feel
like it isn't.

Your voice is a weapon and a bandage and a scar.

Your voice is a key. An open door. A survival tactic.

DON'T HOLD YOURSELF
BACK FROM LOVE.

STARS ARE BRAVE
FOR FALLING.

So are you.

It is BRAVE
to keep your heart
SO OPEN.

Everything is unknown
but the unknown doesn't have to be scary.
It can be full of possibilities
if you're willing to give up
a little control.

You are *not* tied to
anything you have outgrown.

You owe **NOTHING** to
what holds you down.

The amount of time
someone has been a part of your past
has no bearing on whether
they deserve to be a part of your future.

You can't run away from your problems
but sometimes the only way to deal with them
is to put distance between them and yourself.
Give yourself time to breathe and space to think.
That space never has to be permanent.

UNTANGLE YOUR ALONE
FROM YOUR _lonely._

THERE'S PEACE AND
 IN IT.

THERE'S

_breathing
room._

Romantic love is sweet and brilliant

and it makes for good poetry

but it is not the only important thing in your life

and it has nothing to do with your value as a person

or your capacity for happiness.

Treat your body

like a thing that should be protected

instead of a thing that should be whittled down.

Offer it respect and patience and forgiveness.

Stop wishing it away.

Stop trying to magic it smaller.

Allow it space to exist.

Bless the carbs in my morning bagel.

Bless the extra cream cheese.

Bless the unskipped meals,

    every appetizer and dessert.

Bless the dumpster that holds my diet books.

Bless the calorie-counting apps, deleted.

Bless the body, joyous and soft and full.

I want to be understood. I want to be heard. I want all of my feelings to end up where someone can see them. I want to be loved. I want to be wanted in a way that feels safe. I want to be safe. I want to not feel crushed under the weight of my own loneliness. I want to stop needing other people to feel good about myself. I want to need other people. I want to feel good about myself. I want to trust my parents. I want to trust myself. I want to understand the path I'm on. I want to know my future. I want to know why I'm here. I want to know what's really important. I want to understand what I'm feeling. I want other people to understand what I'm feeling. I want to have a big, brilliant life. I want to not feel selfish for wanting a big, brilliant life. I want to be here, really be here. I want people to know I'm here. I want to make an impact. I want to do good things. I want to live quietly and be nobody and be somebody all at the same time. I want to trust the world I'm living in. I want to look at the sky at night and not feel insignificant.

I WANT MY LIFE TO BE

strange

AND

wild

AND

lovely.

I WANT

EVERY

IMPOSSIBLE

THING.

There will be days you drag yourself through
and there will be days you sprint through.

Either way, you're coming out on the other side.

I'm **NOT** here
to justify
   the pain.

I'm here to work
   THROUGH it.

HOROSCOPES FOR LETTING GO

Aries: You gave it your everything. It didn't work out. That doesn't mean it was a defeat or a failure. You don't have to keep trying to do the math and get it right. It's okay to walk away.

Taurus: You're not losing a part of yourself with the relationship. Unclench your fists.

Gemini: Not everyone will stay a part of your life forever.

Cancer: Take off your rose-colored glasses. You can't look at everyone through the lens of love and expect to make clear and balanced decisions.

Leo: Not everything is going to be on your terms. You can't win a breakup by preventing it. Having the last word isn't what's important. Prioritize your well-being over your ego.

Virgo: Everyone makes bad decisions. Sometimes even you. Not everyone is going to turn out to be who you thought they were. Not every relationship is going to go the way you planned.

Libra: Is it really better to be comfortable than it is to be happy?

Scorpio: People don't belong to you. They operate independently of you and your wants and your desires. You can manipulate them into staying, but it's only going to make things worse in the long run.

Sagittarius: Make new memories to sit on top of the old ones. If your favorite place reminds you of an ex, take your friends there. Reclaim what you can and leave behind the rest.

Capricorn: This rocky relationship is not the only one you will ever have or even the best one. You will not be alone forever if you leave it. People are always working toward finding each other.

Aquarius: Love isn't like the movies. It's warm and full and real. Make sure you're not holding out hope for something fantastical and unrealistic. Not everything gets a happy ending.

Pisces: Yes, you opened up and shared your secrets with someone. No, that doesn't mean they have to stay forever.

There is
NO SHAME
in being the most
FEARSOME
thing in the
garden.

Nobody knows how many stars are in space.

Nobody knows how many stars are in me.

On the bad days, be soft with yourself.

On the good days, forgive yourself for the bad days.

My life is going to be full of people and joy and love, regardless of who stays in it and who doesn't.

I will not be afraid to look my mistakes in the face. I don't want to wear the same frown as my mother. I don't want to be another name on the list of angry women in our family. I don't want to inherit their ghosts or fill their shoes or share their stories. I want to tell my own.

NOT everything
OUR PARENTS
TEACH US IS
true, OR
good, OR
right.

~~THINGS MY MOTHER DID NOT MEAN TO TEACH ME~~

REWRITES

you are ▇▇ good ▇▇▇▇

you are ▇▇ enough

My tenderness is _NOT_
an obstacle to
overcome.

GOOD TIMES TO LEAVE
PLATONIC RELATIONSHIPS

When you feel exhausted after talking to them. When you no longer trust them. When they only talk about themselves. When they don't value your time. When they stop putting effort into the relationship. When they don't respect your boundaries. When they don't respect your identities. When they don't respect your well-being. When you stop growing together. When they manipulate you. When they don't share or agree with your morals or values. When you fight more than you talk. When any kind of abuse occurs. When taking care of yourself means leaving. When you want to.

GOOD TIMES TO LEAVE ROMANTIC RELATIONSHIPS

When you feel lonely in the same room as them. When you feel underappreciated. When you feel unsafe. When you start imagining a future for yourself without them in it. When you feel like you can't depend on them anymore. When they hurt you. When you hurt them. When you end up more in love with who they could be than who they are. When you each have different goals for the relationship. When it gets easy to be mean to them. When you argue more than you talk. When you don't feel good around them. When taking care of yourself means leaving. When you want to.

ON HEARTBREAK

Make the space you allow it
smaller and smaller until
you barely remember
the ache at
all.

I AM STILL GOOD.

I AM STILL SOFT.

I AM STILL LOVING.

I AM STILL TENDER.

Even when I'm walking away.

Maybe anything

can be molded into

a _beginning_.

I'm growing with an ACHE in my chest, but I'm STILL GROWING.

That's what counts.

Nostalgia is a wet sundress sticking to my legs. A voice on the other end of the phone whenever I pick it up. A school report on the career path of a novelist. Hot tea with cream and sugar and two drops of red food coloring. Nostalgia is a Popsicle melted in my lap. Pansies potted on a deck overlooking the bay. Cracking my heart like a crab shell and poking around the insides. Guts spread all over the table. Glancing back but still moving forward.

why do you fight with your mother so much?

there are so many things she wants me to be that have nothing to do with who I am / she laughs when I tell her important things so I no longer tell her important things / I don't want to apologize for the parts of me that I can't change / I'm still trying to heal from things she doesn't want me to talk about / the apple didn't fall far from the tree but it tried to / it's hard to look at yourself in the mirror when you don't like what you see / she wanted my life to be better than hers but she didn't know how to tell me that / some part of her still wants to be my hero and I want to be my own hero

Guilt

is what I'm

giving up

today.

some days I feel more honeysuckle than girl.
in the last year I have watched
the best and worst parts of my life
get uprooted.

nothing looks the same anymore.

HOW I TOLD MY PARENTS
I WAS MOVING

I tried as hard as anyone can try
for a thing they don't really want.

I stayed as long as anyone can stay
in a place they don't really belong.

I'm not letting you go

LIKE YOU WERE NOTHING.

I'm just

LETTING YOU GO.

Not EVERYTHING
has to be
CUT and RUN
but I'm SO TIRED
of having my
STRINGS
PULLED.

I WAS NEVER
ENOUGH
for you

BUT I WAS
ALWAYS ENOUGH

for me.

Let me be the start of something new.

Let me live according to that.

An origin instead of a pattern.

Absence makes the heart bitter, cold, and wet:

leaking like a busted pipe

in someone's basement apartment.

A lonely tenant

learning to clean up its own messes,

absence makes the heart grow self-reliant.

WHEN THE EX SHOWS UP

God knows I was loud when you left me. I kept the neighbors up, wailing at night. I cracked the bones of your absence between my teeth until I got used to the taste. I took the space I'd made for you inside myself and I filled it with other people's hands. I moaned your name in my sleep.

Now you have the audacity to bloom on my doorstep again like some cheap metaphor for spring. You rise from the ashes of my mistrust and you do this unforgivable thing: you still make me go soft in the middle.

But it's not enough anymore to draw the blush from my cheeks and scatter my words across the porch. It's not enough anymore to stand there with fresh flowers and wilted apologies.

I don't want someone who comes back. I want someone who stays.

LOOKING FORWARD

I had a dream that someone
asked me to describe love and I didn't
talk about you. That terrifies me—
to think that somewhere out there
in the future might be a version of me
who doesn't think about your lips
when she bites into peaches.
I want to cry thinking about it, but
I also want to be her. I want to crawl
inside her chest and grow until I fit into
her. I want a future for myself where
I am the only one who haunts me.

I'm so sick of reducing lovers to lessons:

How to let go.
How to stay.
How to ask for what the heart wants.

My life is still
BIG and LOUD and
vibrant
when I'm _not_ in love.

It is not my job
to love the harshness
out of other people.

I am the tenderness
that comes with good love,
not after it.

I AM NO LONGER

IDLY WAITING FOR

joy.

POEM IN WHICH I GIVE MYSELF CLOSURE

I know I placed a lot of blame on you at the end
but it wasn't all your fault
and I forgive you for the things that were.

If you need it,
I forgive you for whatever you need forgiveness for.

Not everything
is a metaphor
for **YOU**
and **ME**.

I see your face in other people's faces
not because I'm looking for you everywhere
but because I forget / I forget the things
that made you different from everybody else.

I LOOK BACK
AT THE OLD LOVE POEMS
AND I DON'T RECOGNIZE
THE PERSON
WHO WROTE THEM.

The songs that used to **MAKE ME CRY** don't even make me SAD.

It's not that I don't think about you anymore.
It's just that I don't let it affect my life.

I miss you   and then I make coffee and run errands.
I miss you   and then I go sit in the sun.

I spent SO MUCH TIME
wanting to be

LOVED

that I DIDN'T CARE
if it was

done right.

I don't need you
coming along and thinking you can pull flowers
out of the pit in my stomach.
I am not always pretty and I am not always kind.
I will rip apart the next man who tries
to make the mess of me
into something delicate and mild.

I REFUSE TO TREAT *another relationship* LIKE A **Band-Aid** ON THE SCRAPE OF MY EMPTINESS.

Whoever I love next will know
    I am ready for them,
that they are more than a buffer
    between me and my sadness.
Together we will build a house
    that trauma cannot live inside.

Maybe the trick to not filling the void in my life
with other people
is to build a life I'm not ashamed of living alone.

BRIEF LIST OF GOOD THINGS TO FILL YOUR LIFE WITH OTHER THAN LOVE

Sunsets. Stargazing. The dream of a home with a garden. Tomato plants. Sunshine. Strawberry ice cream. New tattoos. Road trips. Mangos. All the books you haven't read yet. Days spent at the beach. Violets. Saltwater. Plane tickets. Poetry.

Old love is
asking you to
let it go

I do not have to

love my body.

I have to make

~~peace~~ with being

inside it.

I don't remember not hating my body. This doesn't have to be a poem; it can just be a fact. I don't remember not hating my body and yet I know there was a time when I did not hate my body. I know I was not born hating my body. I know I was taught it, like ballet or the violin. I know it was an acquired skill. I know it took years of practice to hate it just right. To hit all the right notes, to know Good Food versus Bad Food, to know how to mask the smell of vomit in the bathroom, to know how to laugh off suspicion. First I made an enemy of the mirror and then I made an enemy of myself. I don't remember not hating my body and yet I know that if it was learned, it can be unlearned.

Earth hips.

Space hips.

Hips like Saturn's rings.

Hips with a gravitational pull.

Hips all about expansion.

Wide hips.

Canyon hips.

Show-me-you've-been-here hips.

Carve-your-name-into-me hips.

Hips all about tourists.

Baby-bearing hips.

Start-a-family hips.

You-need-to-start-a-family hips.

You-really-need-to-start-a-family hips.

You-don't-want-to-wait-too-long hips.

You-don't-want-to-let-your-mother-down hips.

Hips that don't care about letting your mother down.

Stretch-mark hips.

Cocoa-butter hips.

Don't-remind-people-you-are-growing hips.

Dress-for-your-body-type hips.

Don't-dress-for-your-body-type hips.
Hips that don't always tell the truth.
Hips that lie sometimes.
Carnival-mirror hips.

Hips that say NO NO NO
instead of
okay.

I SPENT TOO LONG TRYING TO BE NICE ABOUT IT

The first time a man slapped me on the ass, I was fourteen years old, busing tables at a family restaurant. He asked where I went to college and laughed. I tried to laugh too, but the sound got caught in my throat. I hadn't even been kissed for the first time. He wrapped his arm around my waist, hand warm on the place my shirt rode up—and frowned when a waitress shooed him away. She told me that customers were always right, so I had to be polite, but I could still say *no* if I did it quietly.

When I learned that *no* did not always stop slipping lips and wandering hands, I was told it was my fault for being tempting, and it felt like the truth. I threw out my miniskirts and I apologized.

The second time *no* did not stop someone, I was sitting in the passenger seat of a pickup truck with the doors locked and my dress ripped. I cried later to my mother about it, and she asked if he had been drinking. She said, *you know how men can get sometimes*. She made it sound so inevitable.

The third time was only a few months later. Always on the lookout for bad men, I was blindsided by other genders. No one told me how silent abuse could be or how it could paint your nails and go with you to Pride. How it could pin you down afterward and smile.

It took years for me to realize that only I had a right to my body. I used to bite my tongue, but I do not say *NO* quietly anymore. I bark my distress. I shriek my discomfort. I leave any situation that makes me nervous. I leave any person who makes me uneasy. I never apologize for it.

I PEELED

Shame

OFF THIS BODY

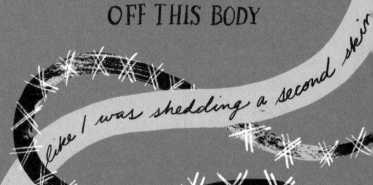

like I was shedding a second skin

THERE IS NO LONGER
ROOM FOR IT
HERE.

I have survived
unthinkable things.

I am not afraid
to do it again.

I remind myself daily
that there are so many things
to make art about
other than
sadness.

Seeds do not sprout
into trees overnight.
The slowness of growth
can be infuriating
but everything
takes time.

We all heal
at our own paces.

I used to shrug off the idea of hope chests, glory boxes, bottom drawers full of baby clothes and magazine clippings of pots and pans. I thought it was a secondhand travesty, a mess of mothers teaching daughters how to be mothers, not how to be people. I thought that would never be me.

My mother gave me a hope chest and I left it empty. I sat it in the back of my closet. I thought, *you can't teach me to be like you. You can't teach me to want things I don't want.*

Now I have a dream board covered in tea kettles and rice cookers, you know, for *later.* I have a pile of travel brochures under my bed. I realized that every book I buy that doesn't have room on a shelf is just waiting for that dream bookcase in a place of my own. I met a girl in Melbourne whose hope was too big for a chest. She had boxes in her family's garage full of teapots and measuring cups and everything she was going to line her apartment with one day.

I'm starting to think that my whole room might be a hope chest for a writing desk and a kitchen of my own. Space of my own. The other day I bought a duvet cover for a king-sized bed and tucked it away in the back of my closet. Even on the days I don't want it to, my whole life reeks of hope for a future where I get out of bed in the morning instead of the afternoon and I match my socks and I always make time to cook my own meals.

I think that the first step to loving the life you have made for yourself is knowing that you want it; and I have a heart bursting at the seams with wanting, lungs full of unused air. I love other people with every inch of myself. My whole life is a hope chest.

The person you are
at the

beginning

of a story

is rarely who you are
at the

end

of one.

STARGAZING PART 2

Now

I bring the sky inside at night.

I stick stars   to my bedroom ceiling

and let myself be
comforted

by the glow.

I make my own
constellations.

Poets are always writing about stardust,
but I spent most of my life feeling like dirt.
I hated that until I realized
dirt is where things have to be planted
in order to grow.

I am living and breathing and creating.

Look at all the things I can do with my hands.

Look at the healing I have written into being.

Look at my voice on the page.

Strong. Resilient. Unaccompanied.

Someone told me once that if I asked for what I needed, the universe would bring it to me; if I lost my way, the universe would guide me; and if I needed a place to land, the universe would catch me.

I am MY OWN
universe.

ACKNOWLEDGMENTS

Thank you to Charlotte Crawford for teaching me all about yelling at the stars.

Thank you to my poetry family for the constant stream of love and support. Thank you to Summer Webb and Caitlin Conlon and Amanda Lovelace for reading and rereading this book.

Thank you to my amazing agent, Penny Moore, and to my wonderful editing team, Sara Sargent and Sasha Henriques. Thank you to Jessica Cruickshank for the beautiful cover and interior illustrations. Thank you to Random House Children's Books for giving this collection a home.

And thank you for reading, always.

ABOUT THE AUTHOR

Trista Mateer is a visual artist, poet, and writer currently based in Maryland. She began putting words on paper at twelve and never found a good enough reason to stop. She is the author of multiple poetry collections, including *Aphrodite Made Me Do It* and *Honeybee*. When she's not writing poetry or telling stories, she is most likely to be found chasing her cat, reading about faeries, or Googling cheap airfare.

tristamateer.com

@tristamateer

ABOUT THE ILLUSTRATOR

Jessica Cruickshank is an Australian illustrator based in Kitchener, Ontario. While Jess draws all sorts of things, her specialties are lettering and typography—her obsession started when she was ten years old, reading the handwritten pages in *The Baby-Sitters Club*. In her spare time, she might be found annoying her dog, embroidering bandannas for other people's dogs, bingeing Netflix, or reading.

jesscruickshank.com
@jesscruicky